Also by Amelia Littlewood
Death at the Netherfield Park Ball
The Mystery of the Indian Diadem
The Peculiar Doctor Barnabus
The Apparition at Rosing's Park
The Shadow of Moriarty
The Adventure of the King's Portrait
The Case of the Patriarch

Copyright © 2018 Amelia Littlewood
All rights reserved.
Published by Cyanide Publishing
www.cyanidepublishing.com

First edition
No part of this book may be used or reproduced in any manner whatsoever without the prior written permission of the publisher, except in the case of brief quotations embodied in reviews.

This is a work of fiction. Names, characters, businesses, places, events and incidents are either the products of the author's imagination or used in a fictitious manner. Any resemblance to actual persons, living or dead, or actual events is purely coincidental.

ISBN: 9781980848844

FROM THE JANE AUSTEN NOVEL
Pride & Prejudice

THE CASE OF THE PATRIARCH

A Sherlock Holmes & Elizabeth Bennet Mystery

AMELIA LITTLEWOOD

CYANIDE PUBLISHING

Chapter One:
Homecoming

There is nothing quite like the English countryside.

While London had become my adoptive home and I had come to love it, I confess that nothing gives me quite the feeling of truly breathing as does the fresh air around Longbourn. I had grown up outside of a small town and I think that will always be where my body is most attuned, the most at peace.

London was full of people of all walks of life, from the meanest and poorest to the highest and most mighty, and people came in from all corners of the British Empire. It was a wonderful place and I loved getting to know every part of it. But I was also excited to come home and pay a visit to the place where I had grown up.

My visit was not entirely cheerful. Father had taken ill, and Mother was in her usual hysterics about him dying and her getting kicked out by Mr. Collins and my dear Charlotte. Personally, I thought that Father had been looking rather frail lately, but it wouldn't do to say that to Mother. It would only cause her to grow even more agitated.

It was decided between Jane, myself, and Charles, my brother-in-law, that I should take Mary and return home to Longbourn to check upon Father. I was Father's favorite, although I myself hated to think of it that way. I have always believed that it is not so much that I am his favorite as it is that we think rather alike, and therefore he sees himself in me. After Lydia's horrid experience with Mr. Wickham and her subsequent subdued behavior, I think that Father had grown fonder of her and Kitty. And I think, truly, that he and Mary would have much to speak of if I could lock them in a room together.

But Kitty and Lydia were thriving in London, and I had confided to Jane that I saw many a young man drawing close to the point of asking for one of their hands in marriage. Georgiana Darcy had become a great friend of theirs and she, too, I had seen waited upon by many a gentleman. They all three made quite a picture, Georgiana with her fine, light blonde hair and sweet face, Lydia with her shock of dark hair and snapping eyes, and Kitty with her soft curls and bright smile.

It would be unfair to them, we reasoned, to take them away from such festivities and suitors when we were not even sure how serious Father's condition was.

Mary, however, jumped at the chance to escape London. Mr. Holmes and I had been spending time with her and she had been assisting him on his Moriarty case, but I suspect that every day reminded her of what she could not have, and what she could not be. She watched the businessmen and lawyers go about their business every morning, and I could see the way that her hands clenched in her skirts.

To think that once my sisters had been such annoyances to me, and that I had cared so little for their thoughts and feelings. Now I felt quite keenly for all of them.

Jane was feeling quite well enough now, she insisted, that she could accompany the three young ladies to balls about town. I was still worried about her condition, but baby Tom, my nephew, was finally sleeping through the night, and Charles confessed that he was longing to spend more time with him. And so it was decided: Mary and I should return to Longbourn and report on Father's condition.

It was fortunate timing, for it was spring and Easter Sunday would be upon us. Always a family holiday, it would please both my parents, I knew, to have at least some of their children in the house.

We took a carriage back to Longbourn, stopping in Meryton to pay our respects to my aunt and uncle, Mr. and Mrs. Phillips. Mrs. Phillips, my mother's sister, was rather like Mother in temperament. That is to say, she gossiped. She did not have Mother's hypochondria, at least, thank heavens.

"Take a look around you," I instructed Mary as we walked through Meryton. "Tell me, what do you see?"

"The fishmonger is courting someone," Mary replied, keeping her voice low. "He's just shaven and his fingernails are neat and trimmed. Not easy for someone of his profession."

"Very good. And the lady over there?"

Mary watched for a moment. "She's put lifts in her shoes to make herself taller. You can tell by the way she doesn't bend her knees as she walks. She's also shoplifting. She's looking around too much and the bracelet she has on doesn't match the rest of her outfit in coloring or style. She must have slipped it on in the shop."

"You might want to warn her." I had learned from experience that if you confront criminals on their actions and then let them off with a warning, they are apt to be frightened enough not to try again. Mr. Holmes had relayed a similar incident to me concerning a Christmas goose.

I watched as Mary went over to speak to the woman. I saw the lady's face register alarm, and then consternation and shame. After a moment she nodded, taking the bracelet off her wrist and handing it to Mary. Mary then took it into the jeweler's.

"Nicely done," I said when she returned to me.

"I don't see why we couldn't just turn her in."

"And what good would that have done? She won't try something like that again and now her poor family has been spared a scandal. A crime affects more than just the victim and the criminal, remember that." What had been done, or almost done, to Lydia had affected all of us, for example.

Longbourn was much the same as I remembered it. Stepping inside was like putting on a pair of comfortable house slippers.

"My darling girls!" Mother said, hurrying to embrace us. I wisely held my tongue about the fact that she had never called us such when Kitty and Lydia and Jane were around. Kitty and Lydia had always been her favorites, and Jane's beauty earned her a special place in Mother's heart.

"Where is Father?" I asked as Mary went to make sure the pianoforte was still in tune. Only she ever played it.

"Upstairs, lying down. Oh, he is near to his death bed, Lizzy, I feel it grow closer every day." Mother shook her head, her hands twisting around and around one another. "And I shall be thrown out of the home I have lived in for almost three decades. And where shall I go? I shall only be a nuisance to Jane, I just know it. She shall grow tired of me."

"You are fine, Mother," I said. "And Father will be as well. Nobody shall be a burden to anybody. Why don't you go check on dinner with the servants, and I shall see to Father."

"Oh, yes, I invited a dear friend for dinner," Mother said. For a moment my heart sank. It must be another suitor, I thought. It had to be. While she had resigned herself to my detecting work with Mr. Holmes, I doubted that she had given up on seeing me married soon.

But to my surprise, Mother then said, "She is a dear girl. Older than you are, Lizzy, but much younger than myself. Her elder sister and I were the greatest of friends growing up. She married into that Lawton family, you know the one, they live quite on the other side of the county."

"I vaguely recall the name, yes."

"Good. See to your Father, now, and do remember your manners when you meet her. She is a dear woman."

"I always remember my manners," I muttered childishly.

Mother gave me a disbelieving look. "I am certain that you think you do. Now run along!"

Father was upstairs in bed, as Mother had said. He smiled when I entered, and I quickly crossed the room to take his hand.

"My dear Lizzy," he said. "How good it is of you to come and see me, and over such a trifle. It is nothing but a cold."

"It was enough to send Mother into fits. For her sake, at least, we had to stop by." I squeezed his hand. "I do worry about you, Papa," I admitted.

"You shouldn't," Father replied. "Worry about yourself instead, my dear. You are up to many a dangerous game lately. And without a husband to back you up."

I didn't want to get into an argument about it, and besides, I knew Father wasn't disappointed in me. He just wanted to look out for me, as a father should. "Are you quite well enough to come down to dinner?" I asked.

"Have it sent up," Father replied. "Your mother is having a friend over in any case and I am certain I want to miss that."

I laughed. He did seem frailer than usual, but his spirits were not diminished—and spirit, in my experience, counted for more than people gave it credit for in the case of one's health. "Very well then. I shall have the maids send dinner up to you. And I shall read to you before bed, if you like. Just like old times."

"I should like that." Father smiled up at me. "I do miss you, my dear Lizzy. Every day."

I felt a pang of guilt. Technically, I should be home at Longbourn, not gallivanting about London, but London was where my heart and ambitions lay. I just wished I could do both at the same time—be the woman that I wanted to be while also being the daughter that my family needed.

"I'll see you tonight, Father."

I left him happy, resting.

Chapter Two:
A Friend In Need

When I came back downstairs, I found that Mother's guest had already arrived and the two were talking up quite the storm.

"Well you know that Easter Sunday is almost upon us," Mother was saying. "All the local families are coming home to spend time with one another. I'm seeing people that you don't see any other time of year, back to stay with their parents."

"Yes, that's just the thing," the other woman replied. She was pretty in a pale sort of way, like the color had been leeched out of her. "That is, none of us have strayed far except for Peter, he's the third of my brothers-in-law, but we're having an official sort of dinner and all of that. The son of a dear friend of Mr. Lawton will be there. Mr. Lawton, my father-in-law, I mean, not my own Charles Jr."

"I'm afraid I know little of the Lawtons," I said.

"I hope that you shall get to know more of them," Mrs. Lawton replied, for that must be her name. "But oh, I've failed to introduce myself, I'm terribly sorry."

"This is Louisa Lawton," my mother said. "Her elder sister, Maria, and I were quite the girlhood friends. Poor thing died in childbirth years ago. She was, what, seven years older than you are, Louisa?"

"Oh, yes, seven." Mrs. Lawton had managed to preserve her youth quite well, I thought, for she was clearly older than I was but still looked a good deal younger than Mother. She reminded me of Mrs. Gardiner, my aunt who lived in London and who often accompanied me in chaperoning my sisters and Miss Georgiana.

The next hour or so was filled with dinner and Mother and Mrs. Lawton reliving their girlhood years. Mary and I mostly listened, politely asking questions now and again. I could feel that Mary was itching to escape and play the pianoforte or do some reading.

I did not find the conversation to be all that stimulating myself, but I nodded politely and asked questions. There was a part of me that was genuinely curious about what my mother was like as a younger woman.

Once, my father had confided in me his first impressions of her. It had been years ago after a particularly trying day dealing with my mother and I had hidden myself in my father's study to, I confess, avoid her. Father had asked me why I was hiding, and I in turn had asked him why he had married such a trying woman.

My impertinence should probably have gotten me in trouble, but instead, Father just laughed a little and said that Mother had been very pretty, and also very lively of spirit. He had appreciated that, being of a much sterner and more introverted disposition himself.

It had surprised me, for the woman I knew was certainly full of more energy than she liked to admit—and had to be in order to raise five daughters—but liveliness also suggested fun and gaiety in one's manner. My mother had neither. Now I listened attentively, trying to reconcile the woman that I knew growing up with the girlish, fun, lighthearted person that Mrs. Lawton was describing.

After dinner was finished and the food had been cleared, we retired to the sitting room. Mary happily escaped with a book somewhere, while the rest of us were served tea. I inquired about Mrs. Lawton's own family, of which she had not told us much. She and Mother had spoken mainly of their own childhoods and Mrs. Lawton's family from before she had married. But I was curious as to the Lawton family. I had heard somewhat of them, but for neighbors that should have been seen often at Meryton, precious little was known about them and they were seldom seen about.

Mrs. Lawton grew quiet for a moment. I did not need to see her biting her lip to know that she was nervous. The feeling radiated off of her like rays from the sun.

"I must confess that I am not only here to relive old times, although I am always glad to do so," she said, looking over at my mother for a moment before turning her attention back to me.

"Miss Bennet, my father-in-law, Charles Lawton, is...well, may I speak plainly?"

I nodded. I had heard many things in my time with Mr. Holmes and I doubted whatever this genteel lady was about to say to me could shock me.

Mrs. Lawton took a deep breath. "My father-in-law is a horrid man, Miss Bennet. He is, I dare say, tyrannical. Oh, it gives me such pain to speak of him this way. You know how important family is. But I simply cannot go on! And I feel I must warn you if you take up the job I am offering you."

"Job?"

Mrs. Lawton nodded. "Mr. Lawton, you see, my father-in-law, owns a great deal of property overseas in the territories of the Empire, including Antigua. Recently he received a small parcel from that country. He would not at first tell us what it was. He likes his little mind games, you see, he teases his sons most awfully.

"Eventually, however, he told us what the parcel was. Apparently, they are pearls. You should have seen the household's reaction. And he made quite a fuss, talking about what he should do with them, and to whom he should give them. He always talks about how he is not long for this world, Miss Bennet, and it is true that he is rather ill and frail now. They say he was very handsome in his time of course and you can see it in my own husband, Charles Jr. And so, he tells us all about these pearls and his plans—and then not two days later, they go missing."

So this was the job that Mrs. Lawton meant. I had to smother a smile. Other people's misfortunes were not something to express joy over, but I confess that the idea of a case to solve filled me with excitement.

"I had heard of your work with Mr. Holmes from your mother," Mrs. Lawton said. "She spoke so highly of your detecting work in London. When I heard that you were coming down for the Easter holiday, I knew that I must prevail upon you to help me.

"We would prefer the police not be involved, you see, for only the immediate family knew of the pearls. The servants are quite unaware, and the man who delivered the parcel did not know what was in it. Mr. Lawton kept it all quite hush-hush."

"And you're hoping, I'm sure, that if the perpetrator is caught, that it can be sorted out amongst yourselves?" I asked.

This made sense to me. After all, we were not dealing with a hardened criminal, at least as far as I knew. A member of the gentry committing what was probably their first crime would, I was sure, be easily contrite.

"Precisely," Mrs. Lawton said, nodding enthusiastically. "My father-in-law is really being quite, well, beastly about it. But he won't hear a word of anyone being brought in. I think he supposes he can terrorize everyone until somebody confesses to the theft. And then I remembered what your mother said about your work with Mr. Holmes and—well, he's quite celebrated, isn't he, in London—and thought that if I invited you down for Easter Sunday, as the daughter of my dear friend..."

"Then I could investigate for you without raising any suspicions." It was a clever idea. "I would be happy to help you out—but, Mother, won't you miss me at Easter dinner?"

"We shall manage quite well," Mother said. "We shall miss you, of course, but we are obliged to miss you all the time, what with your living in London nowadays. Perhaps you could then extend your visit to us by a day or two by way of making up for it."

It was more generous than I'd thought she'd be about the whole thing, so I acquiesced quickly to her suggestion. "It's quite settled then," I said, turning to Mrs. Lawton. "I shall accompany you to your home, and we shall get to the bottom of this matter."

I could hardly contain my excitement. I had a case!

Chapter Three:
An Unhappy Family

While he was in London and I was in Hertfordshire, I still wished to keep Mr. Holmes updated as much as I could on the events transpiring in the Lawton household. To this end, I wrote him a letter detailing the family members and the unfortunate situation.

Dear Mr. Holmes,
It seems an age since we have last worked together, although I know it to be only a few weeks. Hertfordshire is as quiet and charming as you may recall, although I'm sure when you visited it, you found it to be rather dull compared to London, save, of course, for when we solved the murder of Mr. Wickham.
I am writing you because—although I'm sure it will be of no surprise to you—I have a case. Doubtless you've somehow deduced that already.
A family friend has implored me to come to the house of her father-in-law this Easter when the whole family is assembled in order for me to ascertain who stole some valuable pearls that their father recently acquired. I'm sure you can easily picture my excitement. I must confess, however, that there is no lack of suspects here.

Charles Lawton, for that is the name of the father-in-law, is a most unpleasant man. He despises all his children save one and he makes no mystery of it. I am not sure why he should spoil all his affection upon the one son who has been so wayward while his other three are quite dutiful, but I suppose it is one of the mysteries of the human heart we are destined to wonder about.

His eldest son, named for him, is the husband of our family friend. He's very mild of manner and if I were him, I should have stood up to my father ages ago. It's not that Charles Jr. lacks a spine, I think it's more that he considers any battle he should engage in with his father not worth whatever he might gain from it. Of course, someone like that could find other ways to rebel. He seems nervous all the time—I wonder if it is because of his father alone or because he has stolen the pearls?

Louisa, his wife, I like to think is above suspicion. She's very high-spirited and she told me on the carriage ride over that she wishes her husband would stand up to his father more often. I cannot blame her. If I ever marry a man who is so deferential to what other people want all the time, please, Mr. Holmes, do away with me.

The second son is George Lawton. He's clearly jealous of Charles Jr. He has this way of cutting his eyes over to his elder brother whenever he is speaking. It's as if he's waiting for a chance to trip his brother up. He dresses rather ostentatiously, as does his wife Fanny. The sort of man who likes to show off. His clothes are all quite expensive in material and cut. I suspect however that he is irresponsible with money. There is a forced joviality to his voice when he speaks of his business practices. I think things are going much worse for him than he claims.

As for his wife, there is little to speak on. She is a vain woman, always looking for the closest mirror and then examining herself in it.

The third son that I have previously alluded to, Peter, has only recently returned home from the Indies. He says he's been with the Navy, but I laid to him some questions and he answered them incorrectly. He also does not stand like a Navy man, you know—for you taught me yourself—how they all have the same way of standing owing to the movement of the ship and the rigorous training. My guess is that he is a smuggler or privateer of some kind.

The youngest son is Earnest. He's a very sensitive young man. He is also the most despised by his father. I know that it is not polite to talk of such things, but I suspect that his father thought he was, as they say, the sort of man who visited a molly house. Of course, now he has a lovely fiancée, young Julia, and they're quite devoted to one another, but the damage had already been done. Earnest shrinks his shoulders in, trying to make himself look smaller around his father. I dare say his father was hoping for the opposite—that his abuse would make Earnest stronger and more masculine, but instead it just made him more sensitive and scared.

I feel quite bad for him, to tell you the truth—but like Charles, stealing the pearls might be Earnest's way of getting back at his father from another angle.

His fiancée, Julia Grant, is quite the kind of girl that I like. Strong-willed and spirited. I dare say Lady Catherine de Bourgh would hate her. She's rather open in her contempt for her father-in-law. The others seem to think that she's the thief because of this, which leads me to suspect that she did not. It's rather underhanded, to steal something, and Miss Grant seems *the kind of person to spit in your face rather than hurt you behind your back.*

Oh, there is another man as well, but not a relation. His name is Thomas Hillford. He's apparently the son of Mr. Lawton's childhood best friend. The two men, as I understand it, had a falling out about twenty or so years ago, but Mr. Hillford is now here to learn about his father's childhood. It seems his father, the late Mr. Hillford, died when his son was just a boy and he wishes to know more about his early life. He's a rather affable young man. Almost too affable. But I could be leaping to conclusions about people again, as is my wont.

The trouble is, Mr. Holmes, they all have a good motive. Peter has boasted to me about his gambling, and his siblings were more than happy to share stories of the times he lost big playing Lanterloo. Miss Grant could be defying my expectations and have stolen the pearls to spite Mr. Lawton. Earnest has no money of his own and wishes to leave. You can tell by the way his eyes dart about as though he's looking for an exit. It's almost like an animal. I do feel rather sorry for him.

I have no proof, of course, although if you could look into George Lawton for me at his address of work in London, I should be obliged, but given his clothing and the way he speaks, I should think he is in need of funds. And his wife Fanny's jewels are actually paste imitations. I don't believe that she knows about that; I think her husband has sold the jewels and replaced them with paste without her knowledge. Otherwise I do not think she would brag about them so.

Charles is desperate to get out from under his father's thumb but does not dare stand up to him. And then there is Mr. Hillford. He was there when the pearls were stolen and he could be lying about who he is. I have written to Mary who is to look up the Hillfords and see if this Thomas is who he says he is.

That is all for now. I'm sure you are glad you are not here. There is far too much tension in this house with everybody suspecting everybody. I know that you prefer cases where you don't actually have to deal with the nuisances of humanity and can instead refer to the cold, hard facts and observations. I shall keep you abreast of the developments. We will be going in for Easter dinner shortly. I hope that yours is a merry one as well.

Give my love to Mrs. Hudson.

Sincerely,

Miss Bennet

I finished my letter to Mr. Holmes and prepared to go downstairs to dinner. I was not looking forward to it if I was frank with myself. I dared not say anything out loud, of course, but Mr. Lawton was a most unpleasant fellow and I could almost understand why one of his family members would steal the pearls.

All of the family lived under Mr. Lawton's thumb. He held all of the money and doled it out as he pleased. If anyone wanted anything, they had to ask him. George, the second son, worked and lived in London, but I doubted given his behavior and clothing that he was very good at holding onto his money. Earnest had no income aside from this father's charity that I could ascertain, and nobody could or would tell me what Peter had been up to all of this time abroad.

I had to also admit to myself that Peter's attentions to me were a bit... bothersome. I suppose, being the only lady in the house who was not otherwise engaged to another man, it was natural, but I did not find myself drawn to his cavalier manner. There was also much tension that I could sense between Peter and his brothers—a resentment on the part of Charles and George. Earnest seemed to not notice or care, but Peter seemed to be taking special care to make jibes at his elder brothers, and both brothers responded with prickly words and cold manners.

Everyone was already at dinner when I entered the room. Earnest held my chair out for me and I sat, murmuring my thanks. He was a quiet, sweet-tempered person, truly. But could that kind of person hold in a resentment for so long that it would make them desperate enough to steal?

Charles was standing at the mantelpiece, idly running a finger over one of the china pieces there. "Ah, Miss Bennet."

"Mr. Lawton."

"There's only one Mr. Lawton around here," Charles's father and namesake snapped. "Charles, sit down and stop brooding. You rather remind me of a leech, feeding off the cheerfulness of everyone else."

There wasn't much cheerfulness that I could see, at least not from anyone assembled about me. In fact, most of the people assembled seemed subdued—aside from Miss Grant and Mr. Hillford. They both appeared determined to remain cheerful, although Miss Grant appeared to me to be doing so to defy Mr. Lawton, her future father-in-law, while Mr. Hillford seemed cheerful in order to simply buoy the spirits of everyone else.

"Pray tell me, Mr. Hillford," Louisa said, attempting conversation, "what is it that you do? Your profession, I mean?"

"I am studying law," Mr. Hillford said with an easy, albeit lopsided smile. The left side of his mouth turned up more than the right—an endearing quality, I thought, one that quite probably made him more charming to women. All of the Lawton men were quite handsome, as well. Their father had been able to bless them in looks even if not much else.

"Such an ungentlemanly profession," Mr. Lawton said. "None of my sons should ever be allowed to go into law. Having to mingle with the rabble in such a fashion, to defend criminals or waste one's time arguing to hang them when the choice should be obvious to anyone—my sons have not and shall never have to work in such a way for a living."

"Not all of us are fortunate to have such fathers," Mr. Hillford replied, his smile waning.

"On the contrary, Mr. Hillford, I should say you are quite fortunate," Miss Grant replied.

Earnest reached over and squeezed her hand gently, a silent warning for her to curb her tongue. I could easily see why Mr. Lawton might have looked at his pale son, who was mostly silent and obviously quite meek, and thought that he was the wrong sort of dandy, to use a slang term, but it was also rather obvious to me that Earnest was genuinely in love with Miss Grant and that his father's assumptions about him were wrong.

"George works for a living," Peter said, obviously trying to stir up the pot. He was the favorite son, as had been made clear to me by the way that his father did not fling any barbs at him but rather let him have his say. There was no open affection there—but coming from Mr. Lawton, a lack of insults was probably the equivalent of a compliment or a fond touch on the cheek from a kinder parent.

"Yes, well, George has proven himself to be the greediest of the lot of you," Mr. Lawton replied.

I almost choked on my wine. Such bold words would never have been permitted in polite company at any other table, and yet the others all appeared to be used to it. Well, the others, save for Mr. Hillford, who looked quite as alarmed as I felt.

What an odious man, I could not help but think. And to think that I had once thought Mr. Holmes and Mr. Darcy to be the epitome of the horridness of man! They were practically overflowing with compliments compared to Mr. Lawton.

Fanny, George's wife, looked rather pale. Mr. Lawton caught this and raised an eyebrow. "Yes? Do you have something to say? You've been doing such an admirable job of playing the painted lady for your husband, don't muck it all up now by trying to say something intelligent."

Louisa dropped her fork onto her plate with a clatter. I wished that I could reach across the table and take her hand in a show of sisterly solidarity. While I was not an admirer of Fanny's vain nature myself, my instinct was to protect another woman when she was unfairly treated.

Fanny looked down at her plate, obviously near tears. Mr. Lawton sighed, as though he were disappointed that his daughter-in-law had no backbone. I should have liked to tell him exactly what kind of backbone he himself had—for, in my experience, it is a coward who takes potshots at others in order to puff himself up and help himself feel better about himself and hide his own inadequacies—but I supposed that starting a proper fight at the dinner table would not help me with my investigation.

"Tell me," I said, looking to discover what everyone had been doing at the time the pearls had gone missing, "what do you all like to do in the afternoon, after dinner I mean, for enjoyment? Play cards?"

Mr. Lawton snorted. "As though I would let any of my children do such a thing. Peter has already had heavy losses gambling and George is a nitwit at cards."

"I should quite enjoy a round of bridge," Miss Grant said with defiance in her tone.

"I enjoy playing the pianoforte," Earnest said quietly.

"That sounds lovely," I told him.

"The pianoforte is for the lady, not for the gentleman," Mr. Lawton decreed as if it were Biblical law. "And you wonder, Earnest, why I had such doubts about you."

"You had doubts about all of your sons, it seems," Miss Grant quipped.

"Julia, please," Earnest said quietly.

"Oh, no, let's have it all out, I do love a good row," Peter said, leaning back a bit in his chair. "It's been ages since we've had a proper dust-up, wouldn't you say, Charles?"

"I don't think there's any need for that," Charles said quietly, almost as if he were ashamed that his family was behaving in such a manner in front of guests. I would have been ashamed, as well, if it had been my family. I often had been back when Lydia and Kitty were less concerned with proper behavior and would fling themselves at any man in uniform and Mother still found cause to give me embarrassment, but never had my family behaved in a manner as horrid as this.

"Grow a backbone, for the love of all that is holy, Charles," Mr. Lawton snapped. "And to think that I named you after myself, I should have known better—to think that a man who carries on my name and is my heir should be so spineless and simpering."

Charles grew quite red in the face while his wife grew rather pale. I myself felt embarrassment creeping in, on behalf of all of the assembled Lawton family members.

Was it any wonder that those pearls had been stolen? Perhaps one might claim that Mr. Lawton was being worse than usual because of the theft, but I saw it as no excuse for such behavior, and the way that the others around the table merely ducked their heads and took the abuse told me that this was normal for them—that they were, unfortunately, quite used to outbursts and barbs such as these.

"Father," Charles said quietly, his left hand clenching and unclenching around his fork, "I have stayed at home and done all that you have required of me. I do not think that is a cause for ridicule and shame."

"Trust me, I am aware of the faults and failings of my other children, as well," Mr. Lawton said loftily. "I have done nothing but throw good money after bad where George is concerned. Whether it was his misfortune to marry such a peacock of a wife or his own weakness for fine cloth, I shall never know and I do not care. How dire are your financial straits this time, my dear son? I can only presume that is why you chose to spend Easter with us instead of making some excuse as you did at Christmas."

"My finances are as well as they ever were," George replied, snapping right back at his father. The way his face colored, however, told me that was a lie. Yet, George did not strike me as a man who would rob pearls unless he was certain he would not be discovered. There was no mettle to him, and one needs either a sufficient amount of desperation or mettle to pull off a crime. Was his desperation enough, then, to lead him to steal them?

I had to find out where the pearls were hidden. My plan was that tomorrow on Easter Sunday, when all of the assembled family members were left to their own devices after church, I would record their movements—for it only made sense to me that after a few tense days, the thief should check on the pearls. I had little doubt that the pearls would be taken to be sold on Monday after the holiday, now that a few days had passed, and the stores would be open again.

Tomorrow, then, would be my only chance to find the pearls. I was determined not to fail, if only for the sake of Louisa, but personally, I rather felt that the old man deserved to have something valuable taken from him. Let him know what it felt like to be a victim instead of attacking and victimizing others. But it was not my job to judge my clients, I reminded myself, it was only my job to detect and learn who had committed the crime.

I felt uncharacteristically nervous without Mr. Holmes there, but I was determined to succeed. I would prove to myself that I could handle this case.

Chapter Four:
On The Third Day

Easter Sunday was on the third day of my visit to the Lawtons. I confessed privately to Louisa that I was not at all certain who had taken the pearls, and so a plan was concocted that we arrange for me to search everyone's rooms after dinner while the others had drinks and played bridge.

The thief had to have the jewels nearby, I reasoned, both to make sure they were safe and to have them on hand when the time came to leave—or flee. My suspicions currently rested on either Charles or Earnest. Peter had always asked for money from his father and had always received it. Why would he stoop to theft when he could be reasonably certain that he'd be given whatever money he asked for?

Julia Grant, meanwhile, I did not see as the kind of woman who would go behind someone's back in such a manner. She had been bordering on rude in her behavior towards Mr. Lawton, spurred by her righteous anger over the treatment of her fiancé. I could hardly blame her.

The others, though, I could all too easily see employing theft in order to buy themselves freedom or a way out of a dire financial situation. I tried not to make too many assumptions, for I knew that such assumptions upon a person's character so early in my acquaintance with them had spelled disaster for me before. Yet, as a detective, what could I do except deduce based upon behavior?

I sent my letter off to Mr. Holmes that afternoon and then prepared myself for dinner. As the guest, or one of the two guests, I felt it was important that I look my best and put on a good impression. I had found Mr. Lawton to be as miserable and manipulative as his daughter-in-law had said. It was unfortunate, to be in the presence of such a person. But needs must and I was not about to make Louisa look bad by presenting myself as anything less than a lady.

At this point I would like to say that I do hope the reader will excuse my use of people's first names—it would be too unbearably confusing to call all the men save one "Mr. Lawton" and all the women save one "Mrs. Lawton."

I had been making careful notes of everyone's movements throughout the day. Earnest was downstairs playing the pianoforte while Miss Grant turned the pages for him. Earnest had been at the pianoforte for some time. He and Mary should have got along well. I could hear Miss Grant singing snatches of songs here and there, although not terribly loudly. Possibly she was ashamed of her voice, or perhaps she simply wished not to disturb anyone.

Louisa was overseeing things in the kitchen. I could tell that she was nervous that all should go well. Fanny I had heard go into the room she was staying in with her husband, and from time to time, I heard her barking orders at her maid.

It was a rather quiet day, all things considered. Everyone had been avoiding one other. I could sense this general air of suspicion about the house. Everyone had their own theory as to what was going on and who had taken the pearls. It was not, as one might say, a happy family.

The only disturbance during the day had been a knock at the door about halfway through my letter to Mr. Holmes. I noted the time on the clock—three in the afternoon. Dinner would be in about two hours, I thought, and rose to see who the visitor was.

Louisa invited him in. I caught only a glimpse of him before he entered into the private study of Mr. Lawton.

"That's Lt. Henry Crawley, an officer of the militia stationed at Meryton" she told me in a whisper. "Here about the pearls."

"But I thought Mr. Lawton didn't want anyone to look into it?"

"Perhaps he changed his mind."

I was a little concerned about another investigator being brought in, but I said nothing. It was not my place to question what the head of the household was doing when he didn't even know my true reason for being there.

At five o'clock, everyone was in the same place they had been before. It fascinated me that Fanny Lawton could spend over two hours simply playing dress-up in her room, letting her sister-in-law slave away preparing everything for Easter dinner, which must be even more elegant than usual dinners.

I was just exiting my room to go down the hall when I heard raised voices. I paused, my curiosity getting the better of me.

It sounded like Charles Lawton, the eldest son, and George, his brother. They appeared to be speaking in the drawing room at the bottom of the stairs. I couldn't see either of them, but I could hear them quite clearly.

"This has got to stop. Don't you see that?" Charles was saying.

"Oh, yes, after all this time, you've finally gotten an opinion of your own. Well done brother," George snapped back. "I would congratulate you more heartily, except that it comes at the expense of treating me as if I were a child."

"You are behaving like a child and therefore must be treated like one. A spoilt child, in fact. Father should have refused to bail you out years ago. To mismanage things as you do—"

It was not my place to continue to listen, especially as their conversation seemed to have nothing to do with the pearls. It confirmed for me that George was in financial trouble, and so I passed onward down the stairs and into the main dining room.

Louisa was overseeing the servants setting up some plates. "Oh, Miss Bennet, if you would be so kind as to fetch Mr. Hillford? I'm quite at a loss as to where he might be."

"Certainly." According to my last notes, Mr. Hillford was in the library, reading some old letters that his father had sent to Mr. Lawton when they were children. He hadn't stirred from it, unless he had managed to do so without making the rather loud floorboards of the library, which were directly beneath my bedroom, squeal.

Louisa disappeared through the doorway on the other side of the room.

I had scarcely made my way out of the dining room and into the drawing room when I heard it. The whole household, I believe, had to have heard it, for it was a most awful sound.

It was a scream.

A horrible scream, a kind of wailing scream—and I was suddenly reminded of when I was a child and would hear tales of banshees from Mother's maid, an Irishwoman. The banshees were great, wailing ghosts of women on the Irish moors. I'd never heard one, of course, for such things didn't exist, but if they did, I could well imagine that they sounded just like this scream did.

I froze, and indeed I felt the entire house seem to freeze, everyone pausing to listen to that awful scream.

The moment it died out, in a kind of odd gurgle, I began to run. It was obvious where the scream had come from—Mr. Lawton's quarters, the part of the house that belonged to him and him alone. I had been instructed from the beginning not to go into those quarters, and had adhered to it, but I knew where they were, and specifically, where his study was located.

The door was right between a series of white statues, which Mr. Lawton had bragged to me on the evening before he had brought straight from Italy. I tried the door at once—only to find it locked.

A moment later, I was surrounded by everyone else. The five men—the brothers Lawton and Mr. Hillford—then tried the door.

"It was the most awful scream!" Fanny said, looking quite ready to faint. "It was like—like a squealing pig!"

"Or a soul going to Hell," Julia said, her tone not mean as I would have expected, but awed in a fearful, hesitant sort of way.

"It won't unlock, the blasted thing!" George said, thumping on the door uselessly.

"It's solid oak. I don't see how it should give way easily," Peter pointed out, almost jovially, as though this was a game.

"The bench outside of the kitchen," I said. "There is one, is there not? I saw the cook shelling peas there yesterday morning. It ought to serve as a kind of battering ram, oughtn't it?"

The men hurried and procured the bench, which was used posthaste to burst open the door.

There was a knocking at the front door, but I was certain that I was the only one who had noticed it. The others were all staring into the room—and well they should stare, for it was a sight.

Poor Mr. Lawton was lying on the floor, his throat slit. Blood was absolutely everywhere. It glistened a bit in the dying light of the sun. It was enough to make a person ill, even me, and I had seen death and violence before.

The knock sounded at the front door again.

"I'll get that," I said. "Louisa, you must get the other women into the drawing room, please. There's no need for them to see this. Gentlemen, do not touch anything."

"And you speak with such authority because?" George Lawton asked.

"Because I am the partner of Mr. Sherlock Holmes, the London detective," I said. "And if you would be so kind as to listen to me, I can help you figure out who did this, or at the very least, prevent you from destroying the evidence of the crime scene."

I then hurried to the front door.

When I opened it, I saw to my surprise that it was Lt. Crawley. "Lieutenant," I said. "I had thought your business here was conducted."

"It was, but I—good Lord, what is all the fussing?" he asked, looking over my shoulder and seeing Louisa and Julia leading a weeping Fanny into the drawing room. The woman's nerves were either quite frail or she was putting on a bit of a show for everyone.

"We've had a terrible occurrence," I said, knowing that if I lied, the truth would only come out through some other means. "Mr. Lawton, the man of the house, has just been murdered."

"Murdered? Good Lord." Lt. Crawley stepped inside and strode over to the men. "When did this happen?"

"Just now," I said. "There was a scream and then we found him in his study."

"I shall have to see it at once."

"It was a horrid scream," Fanny said. "Not a proper human scream at all. A devil scream, like the devil he was!"

"Please, Fanny, do calm down," Louisa implored.

"Who had the keys to the room?" Peter asked.

"I did," Charles said, the eldest. "And my wife."

"But I do not have them on me, they always hang by the door, anyone could have locked it," Louisa said.

Earnest hurried out of the room. A moment later he returned, keys in hand. "They were on the nail as they are usually," he said, "but it would be the work of a moment to pick them up and then return them. I don't think that any of us use them regularly."

"You have your own set on you at all times, do you not?" Lt. Crawley demanded of Charles.

"Yes, but—why on earth should I have reason to kill my father?" Charles spluttered.

"Oh, come now," Peter said, leaning nonchalantly against the fireplace. "I hate to speak ill of the dead, but Father was a rotten old—"

"There are ladies present," Charles reminded his brother.

"—egg," Peter finished.

"He was rotten," Earnest admitted. "He was a beast. But there's no reason to talk about it now, not now that he's dead."

"On the contrary," I said.

37

Everyone looked at me.

I cleared my throat, feeling a little self-conscious now that everyone in the room was staring at me. "Somebody killed Mr. Lawton. It's now important that we figure out who. That can only happen if we talk openly and honestly about what we know of him and how we felt about him and the facts of the day."

George snorted. "As if we should talk about such things—and with whom should we speak of them? You? I mean no offense, Miss Bennet, but last I was aware, it was far from the realm of a lady to investigate such gruesome matters as these."

"Miss Bennet is a detective," Louisa said, standing up and squaring her shoulders. "She is here at my request. She works with the great Mr. Holmes in London, as she said before. I asked her to come so that she might discreetly look into the matter of the stolen pearls."

Charles walked over to the mantle, gently rearranging an ornamental teapot sitting on it. "My dear, you failed to inform me of this."

"You could hardly keep a secret if you were paid to do it, Charles," Louisa replied. "I thought it best that as few people as possible know of Miss Bennet's true errand in visiting us."

Charles moved away from the mantelpiece—rather quickly, I noted. "Well, I don't see what good she could do for us now."

"Surely you would rather have her investigate than drag the police into this," Louisa said.

"Miss Bennet has my vote," Julia piped up.

"She'll get no assistance from me," George said. I really should have expected such resistance from the men. Earnest didn't look too resistant to the idea, but the other three brothers and Mr. Hillford all appeared rather agitated—I could tell by the way that their left fists clenched at their sides.

"Really, my dear brother," Peter said with a smile, chuckling a little behind his hand. "There's no reason to be quite so put out about the whole thing—unless of course you were the one to do it? What were those money troubles that Father so kindly brought up at dinner yesterday?"

I saw Earnest and Mr. Hillford flash lopsided smiles, the left-hand sides of their mouths turning up—but quickly they smoothed their faces into seriousness when George looked at them.

"I can conduct interviews, as to everyone's whereabouts," I said. "I can start with the ladies if you'd like."

"You'll do no such thing," George replied.

"Perhaps I could help," Lt. Crawley said quietly. "It might be that the men will take me more seriously—no offense meant to yourself, Miss Bennet, but you know how some people can be."

I supposed that there could be no issue in that. Lt. Crawley was a military man, and in my experience, such people were generally automatically respected. I nodded at him, and Lt. Crawley gave me a small smile.

"Gentlemen, please," he said, stepping forward. "If you should be so kind as to follow me, I would like to take your statements. If we can all cooperate, this

39

will be much easier for the police and they will have less involvement—which I am certain is what you all would prefer."

"Perhaps the ladies would like to go on a walk to Meryton," I said. "I have a letter to post anyway. And some fresh air, I should think, will do us all some good."

"Oh, that does sound wonderful," Miss Grant said. She took the pale Fanny by the hand. Fanny still looked to be in quite a bit of shock from the whole ordeal. "Some shopping about the town will do you some good, won't it? I shall pay, of course," she added quickly, most likely upon seeing the thunderous expression on George's face.

George chuckled amicably behind his hand, as if to cover up the anger he had been exhibiting the moment before. "Of course, you ladies would need something to work off your shock."

"Then it's settled," Louisa said. "We shall go into Meryton, and the gentlemen shall speak to Lt. Crawley."

"Go on and get ready," I said.

Everyone dispersed, and I took the opportunity to quickly re-enter the study.

The matter of the blood concerned me. There was so much of it. Why on earth would someone go to all the trouble of splattering all that blood?

I checked the carpet most minutely, but there was nothing that the blood was hiding, no message or secret pattern in the rug or piece of paper that the blood was covering up. There was nothing…

Except...

I peered down. By the window, which was ever so slightly ajar—but not large enough for someone other than perhaps a small child to climb through—there was a small piece of rubber on the floor.

I picked it up and examined it. It was a rather thin piece of rubber, light pink in color. It felt flimsy, but it had a bit of stretch to it. What could it have been used for? Surely it did not belong to anything in the study. There was no large piece of rubber or furniture that it could have come off of, and it did not belong to an article of clothing. I supposed that it might have blown in from the outside...but surely that was ridiculous. No, it must have something to do with the murder.

When I returned, the ladies were all assembled, and we proceeded onto the walk.

"Horrible!" Fanny declared. "Absolutely horrible! I shall never forget that sound or that sight for as long as I shall live. I am quite inclined to tell George we must leave the house immediately! I cannot spend a night more in there knowing what has occurred and who might still be lurking about to kill one of us next!"

"The old man was murdered because of his horrible nature," Miss Grant replied. "I doubt that you shall be the next target, or indeed that any of us shall. What have any of us done to provoke one another? We were all trapped in that suffocating house with him and he has no one except for himself to blame now that his awful behavior has come back to bite him."

"You really should not speak such ill of the dead," Louisa said quietly.

"And why not? It's true, isn't it? And nobody dared to say it when he was alive to get at them, so we might as well relieve ourselves and say it now in the fresh air."

"George is more like his father than he would like to admit," Fanny said. "He has a temper—but nothing, not nearly as bad, that is not what I mean. I just think… that perhaps the sons did not help when it came to the father."

"Earnest is nothing like his father," Miss Grant said loyally. "Of course, there are the little physical tells, like that smile."

"Such a charming smile," Fanny said. "I quite fell in love with George when he first smiled at me like that."

"And they all have a rather strong fondness for roast chicken with lemon," Louisa added, smiling fondly.

"It is strange, is it not, how all such different people can show the same behaviors—but not in the ways that matter?" Miss Grant mused. "Earnest is gentle as a lamb and I feel I must protect him half the time, if I am honest. And Peter is reckless and jovial, quite the good-natured rogue, if I may say so. Charles is patient. Poor Earnest isn't; he gets quite agitated if his meals are ever served late. None of them are at all like their horrible father, and yet they all laugh the same way and show their irritation in that little hand clench—yet where it truly counts, they are all as different as if they were strangers!"

"No wonder I have been feeling quite confused lately," I confessed. "They all do rather look alike, do they not?" I laughed. "After studying with Mr. Holmes, it is in my nature to observe the small physical ticks of the people around me so that I might understand them. With so many men behaving in a similar manner, it has quite confused me at times. I feel as though I'm seeing things I've already seen."

"Is that so? I never thought of it that way." Louisa laughed. "It is fortunate then that they are all so different in character."

"I cannot believe that one of us would murder Mr. Lawton," Fanny said quietly. "It was a horrible thing." She shuddered. "Horrible. I have found Peter to be bothersome and Earnest is too quiet for me—I beg your pardon, Miss Grant—and yet I cannot fathom any one of them to be a killer. A thief for the pearls, yes, I have wondered who among us could have done that and I quite well think it should be any of us but…to slit a man's throat…"

At that, the conversation fell away. I was wrapped up in my own thoughts about the matter. I had to agree with Fanny, who was surprisingly astute despite her usual self-absorbed manner.

Who among the people assembled was cold-hearted and bloodthirsty enough to be a killer?

"It was fortunate," I said, "that Lt. Crawley was there to assist in the investigation of the pearls. I had thought that your father-in-law did not wish anyone outside of the family to know."

"He said that he came to inquire about a theft," Louisa said. "I can only presume that is what he meant."

That was interesting. "And he did not mention the pearls specifically?"

"Not that I can recall," Louisa replied, speaking slowly as she tried to remember. "No, not that I can think of. I merely assumed that is what he meant, I suppose, for what other theft could he be calling about? Unless there was another theft that we did not know of?"

"He might have been asking after a rash of thefts," Miss Grant said. "There are those professional burglars that move through an area, you know, robbing the various houses before moving on."

Before I could pursue the thought further, however, I heard my name being called.

"Miss Bennet?"

I turned to see none other than Mr. Darcy walking towards me. I confess that I was happier than usual to see him—to have a familiar face in such troubling times was a relief. "Mr. Darcy. I did not know that you were staying in Meryton."

"I am merely passing through on my way to London," Mr. Darcy replied. "Are you visiting your family then?"

"I was, but I am afraid that I am now engaged in a more serious matter." I did not tell him exactly of what, for it was not my place to speak of my clients.

"Oh, Miss Bennet, who is this?" Louisa said, hurrying up.

I quickly made the proper introductions.

"Oh, Miss Bennet is such a help, is she not?" Louisa asked.

"She has assisted me in the past, or rather my aunt," Mr. Darcy replied gravely. "Is she assisting you in a case of your own?"

"Yes, we have had a series of misfortunes lately and Miss Bennet is kind enough to assist us in the matter. We have the utmost faith in her."

"If you wish to proceed with your shopping, Louisa, I would like to catch up with Mr. Darcy," I said, smiling at her.

Louisa nodded and hurried off. The moment that she was out of earshot, I turned to look at Mr. Darcy again. "I cannot disclose to you the details of the case, but I am glad that you are nearby so that I might—if it is not a trouble to yourself, of course—have you on hand to assist me if needs be? I fear that I have far too many suspects and no one in the house that I can truly rely upon. I am not certain that I shall need you, but if I did…"

"Of course," Mr. Darcy replied. "I will be on hand. It is no trouble to stay on for another day or two. Is Mr. Holmes not with you?"

"He is still in London. This case came upon me rather suddenly."

"Ah. Well, I do hope that you will be careful, Miss Bennet. In my experience—limited as it is—those that know too much or are too intelligent are the ones in the most danger when someone wishes to get away with doing something."

His words were wise ones, and it reminded me that I truly could trust no one involved in this case, but that did not curb my determination. I would learn the meaning behind all of the clues and I would apprehend this thief turned murderer.

Chapter Five:
A Near Miss

This case was frustrating me no end. There was so little physical evidence! I felt as though the murderer was laughing at me.

Well, I had allowed myself to be fooled once, by Miss Adler. While she may be excused, I could not allow myself to be so fooled again. I would find out who this murderer was and I would bring them to justice.

Lt. Crawley came up to me as I returned to the house, deep in thought. "Miss Bennet," he said, "I've conducted the interviews at your behest. I've written everything down here in my notebook, if you wish to take a look."

"Yes, I would. Thank you kindly, Lt. Crawley."

I had just taken the notebook from him when there was a crash and an almighty scream.

Then I heard a cry of "Julia!"

I dashed into the house, Lt. Crawley on my heels.

There, at the foot of the stairs, was Julia Grant. She was lying on top of a great pile of laundry, holding her ankle. "Oh," she said, gasping in pain. "Oh, it's quite—it's quite broken, I should think."

Earnest was kneeling beside her, his face white with worry. "How in the world did you manage to fall down the stairs, darling?" he asked, the endearment slipping out in front of others due to his distress.

I turned and looked up the stairs. It was faint, but I thought I could see...

I went up the stairs and there it was—a string, tied across the top stair by use of a nail. "She tripped over this," I said, indicating it.

"Thank goodness for the laundry," Louisa said. "I had just set it down for but a moment. If it hadn't been resting at the bottom of the stairs... to cushion the fall..."

It was a sobering thought. The great pile of laundry was undoubtedly bedsheets, and a great deal of them due to everyone staying in the house. They had saved Miss Grant's life.

"I should like to speak to Miss Grant, if I may," I said. "And if someone would fetch a doctor?"

"I shall," Peter said, hurrying out.

We helped Miss Grant into the sitting room, where I insisted on everyone leaving. Lt. Crawley did not seem happy with this. No doubt he thought us equal partners in the investigation now.

Once we were alone, I turned to Miss Grant. "Julia—if I may call you so?"

She nodded.

"Julia, someone put that there deliberately to try and kill you." I knelt at her feet. "You must tell me the truth about what happened yesterday. There is something you haven't told me, something dangerous to the murderer."

As she sat there, I thought back to what it could have been. What had she seen that I had not?

I put myself back in the moment of the scream. I was in the dining room, just exiting... I ran down the hall, past the four statues...

No, wait.

There were only three statues when Mr. Lawton had boasted of them to me earlier. How could there have been four?

I looked at Julia and I remembered what she had been wearing when we had all entered the study. "Julia," I said, "you were already in the hallway when I got there. You were there before the murder happened."

Julia nodded, tears springing into her eyes. "I only wanted to talk to him," she said. "He was always so cruel to Earnest, and it just made Earnest retreat more, become more sensitive, so that made Mr. Lawton be crueler, and so on and it was all a horrible cycle. I just wanted to—to give him what for and to tell him to leave Earnest alone.

"But when I got there, the door was locked, and there was no answer inside—and then that horrible scream...

"I knew that if I was the first one there, that everyone would think that I had done it. Everybody already thought that I had stolen the pearls. I was quite awful to Mr. Lawton. I made no pretense of my dislike of him. What else would everyone have thought except that I had done it out of spite and to protect Earnest?"

49

I patted her knee reassuringly. "Don't worry, we'll sort this whole thing out."

"I know that you will," Julia said, smiling at me. "You're quite clever, I can tell. But... but Miss Bennet. You must understand. I was in the hallway when the murder happened. Nobody could have gotten out of that room without my seeing them. And yet... nobody came out. Don't you see, Miss Bennet? There was no one *there*..."

This whole thing was rather troubling me, as I'm sure the reader can imagine. I calmed Julia until the doctor arrived to look at her ankle, at which point I stepped back and allowed the family to do their part in comforting her.

"I must admit that I am quite at a loss," Lt. Crawley told me. "But then, in the militia, one rarely has the opportunity to deal with a cold-blooded murder such as this. It's all in the heat of the moment against your enemy on the battlefield. Quite a different sort of danger, one might say."

"Quite," I agreed. "Pardon me. I must find a paper and pen." I had to write to Mr. Holmes of the matter.

"The murderer must have silenced Mr. Lawton for realizing they had stolen his pearls," Lt. Crawley went on. "If we find the thief, then we shall find our killer, I am quite certain, Miss Bennet."

"I'm sure that you are quite certain, sir," I replied, locating a paper and pen and sitting down to write.

Seeing that I was as good as dismissing him, Lt. Crawley finally let me alone to write in peace.

I confessed all facts of the case to Mr. Holmes, including the bit about the blood.

I simply do not understand, Mr. Holmes, why there should be such an excess of blood. It all sounds rather like a theatrical show, doesn't it? The scream, the blood everywhere—too much blood, in fact, for one human being.

Why should someone go to such lengths, such trouble, to pour so much blood upon the scene? It seems rather fantastical to me. I thought perhaps that the blood was done to obscure some other fact, perhaps something about the carpet or some message—but I have checked the room thoroughly and there is nothing.

Thank heavens that London is but a day's ride from Longbourn, for I received a letter in return shortly afterward. We had spent the day looking for the pearls, which no one had as yet confessed to stealing. Bedrooms were, naturally, searched first, but so far, there had been no sign of them. I was feeling quite hopeless.

"I hope you do not feel that I am failing you," I told Louisa. "We shall crack this case, I am quite sure of it. But it might take some time. Few cases are solved in a matter of hours, you know."

"Please, my dear, I asked you down about some pearls, not about a grisly murder such as this," Louisa assured me. "I understand that now you must have many more deductions on your plate than you expected. You shall have free reign to do as you wish in order to figure out who committed this horror."

Mr. Holmes's letter was short and to the point, as was his manner, but contained an interesting note that struck me more fully than the others.

This bit about the blood that you have mentioned rather reminds me of a case that I worked some time ago. A man had taken revenge upon the two men responsible for the death of his sweetheart and her father, and upon killing them had written "rache" in blood upon the wall. This word, as you know, Miss Bennet, means "revenge" in German. This may sound a bit familiar to you. This case was the inspiration for Mr. Hope, the man Miss Bingley hired to kill Mr. Wickham.

The writing on the wall was a completely illogical thing to do. Indeed, it told us the man's motive. Why should he do it, then? Because while we deduce facts, Miss Bennet, there are psychological reasons for why people commit crimes. This man murdered because he felt a wrong had been dealt and he wanted the world to know of that wrong. It seems to me as though this person is the same—there is a message in all that blood. It is a sign of something.

I was inclined to agree. This was a show, a bit of theatricality—but what the message?

What was the blood trying to say?

Chapter Six:
The Wrong End

I wrote back to Mr. Holmes expressing my frustrations.

You must understand that I am quite out of my mind with the lack of physical evidence this case provides. I have narrowed it down to three clues of importance: this bit of rubber that I found at the crime scene, the scream and the locked door, and then the blood.

The door, I have reasoned, was to prevent anyone from entering the room, although why, I cannot fathom. As to the bit of rubber, it reminds me of something, but I cannot yet ascertain as to what. I am going into the market to mail this letter and shall be stopping by a few shops—perhaps there is someone there who can tell me what this bit of material belongs to.

To ensure that all of my bases were covered, I asked Mary to run some errands for me. She was happy to do so in order to assist in the investigation. First, I had her to go check and see that Mr. Hillford was who he said that he was.

Mary found out that he was—and that he had come to Meryton to visit the Lawtons only a few weeks after his mother had passed away. It seemed that Mr. Hillford had waited only until all of his affairs

53

were in order and the funeral arrangements settled before coming to visit his father's childhood friend.

An unusual coincidence—and one that made me feel as though I were missing something. That there was something itching at the back of my mind that I could only as yet graze with my fingertips.

Mary also informed me as to how Father was doing. "He is quite a bit better than he was before when you last saw him," she told me when we met up in Meryton. "I suspect that Mother's fussing has spurred him into greater health in order to get her to let him alone."

"I cannot help but fear that Mother is right and that he is beginning to put one foot in the grave," I admitted. Mother was prone to hysterics, but Father was old. In fact, he was a good ten years older than Mother—her youth, he said, had been part of what had drawn him to her when they first met. With all of his children fully grown, he was getting on in years. I could remember how he used to go for long walks every morning, how now he rarely stirred from his chair.

"Father is fine," Mary said firmly. "I have been looking after him with great care and not allowing Mother to work herself into too great of a tizzy over the matter. We shall be making wedding arrangements for Lydia and Kitty long before we plan for Father's funeral."

I nodded. "Of course, you are right. I should let you get back—I will let you know of any developments in the case. I feel that I am very close to figuring it out… that there are only some things that I should be seeing clearly that I am not, as though I am wearing fogged glasses."

"You will solve it," Mary said, her voice full of conviction. "I am certain of it. All the pieces will fall into place for you in time."

I thanked her and let her go on her way back to Longbourn and set out to wander through Meryton on my own.

Meryton was busy, as usual, and many items that had been stocked for Easter were now marked down so that shopkeepers might be rid of their extra stock. I visited a few shops but was unable to find out what the bit of rubber was used for.

I began to fear that I could not solve the case without Mr. Holmes there. Was it really that I was nothing without him? Could I only be his assistant and nothing more?

I paused in front of a shop for children. Lydia and Kitty were quite old now and had never been interested in such things anyway, but perhaps my little nephew might like something. A stuffed bear, maybe?

Entering the shop, I surveyed the merchandise. There was a darling little stuffed puppy that was quite soft, perfect for a baby. I went to the counter to make my purchase—and that was when I saw them.

Dying Pigs.

I pointed excitedly behind the counter where they hung. "Sir, please tell me, are those popular? They had them when I was a child."

"Ah, yes, quite." The shopkeeper smiled at me. "I make them myself."

I held out my piece of rubber. "Would this be a part of it, do you think? From one that has already been popped?"

"Why yes, miss, that is the same kind of rubber. They rather explode into bits when you let them go. Make quite the horrible sound, don't they? Young boys come in here all the time to buy them as pranks. I shouldn't wonder if there's been many a spanking over these toys."

So, this was what the rubber was—and what had produced the scream! A child's toy! But why should a scream be needed? After all, the door was locked. Surely it would benefit the murderer to ensure that the death went unnoticed for as long as possible? Why alert everyone to it?

I purchased the stuffed puppy and turned to go, only to run straight into Mr. Darcy.

"Miss Bennet." He spied the puppy. "For Thomas, I presume?"

"Yes, I thought he might like such a toy."

"I had rather the same thought." Mr. Darcy held up a small stuffed rabbit. "I suppose there's no harm in spoiling the boy just a little bit."

"I'm sure neither of his parents will object," I said, smiling.

"Tell me, Miss Bennet, how goes the case?"

"More poorly than I should like," I told him. "It is rather frustrating. There are few physical facts, everyone had a motive—and poor Miss Grant was nearly killed—and honestly, Mr. Darcy, I've been having the worst sense of déjà vu ever since I stepped into the place."

"Forgive me for being so frank, but it is not in my nature to make pretty words when honest ones will do," Mr. Darcy said, paying the shopkeeper for the rabbit. "I am not surprised that Mr. Lawton has met such an end. A grislier one than I think anyone dared to imagine, but when I first visited Netherfield with Mr. Bingley to see about his purchasing it, we heard quite a lot about the old man.

"He was a trial to his wife, or so I was told. Had affairs behind her back, although, of course, nobody dared speak of such things when she was alive. It seems she was often ill."

"It makes me sick," I said, "to think of how men so often treat their wives. I am glad that my sister Jane has found such an agreeable and sweet-tempered man as Mr. Bingley, for I shudder to think of what other possibilities there might have been."

"Philandering is not nearly so rare as people would like us all to believe," Mr. Darcy said gravely. "I have heard far too many a man boast of his exploits, and it is often the women who suffer. I shouldn't wonder that there aren't more children born out of wedlock than there are generally acknowledged. And do these men ever suffer for their actions? No. It is the women and the children who do."

I stared at Mr. Darcy. The puzzle pieces were falling into place almost faster than I could handle them. I knew now why I was feeling so strongly that things that were happening to me had happened before, and I knew now why there was so much blood, why it was a murder of blood—and most importantly of all—

"Miss Bennet?" Mr. Darcy asked. He looked rather alarmed. I am certain that my face must have gone quite white. "Are you quite well? Miss Bennet?"

I grabbed his arm. "Mr. Darcy. I have been a fool. I've had quite the wrong end of the case this whole time. You must help me fetch some policemen—I know who the murderer is!"

Chapter Seven:
A Person First

I gathered all the member of the Lawton family, as well as Mr. Hillford and Lt. Crawley, into the drawing room.

"This is rather unorthodox of me, I know," I admitted, "but Mrs. Charles Lawton, Louisa, did ask me here so that I might be discreet. And as this is obviously a family matter, I thought I ought to present the truth to you all first before calling in the police."

Everyone nodded, a few people shifting uneasily in their chairs. It always amazed me by how even innocent people will act nervously or guiltily when in a stressful situation, even if they know they are not the one in trouble.

"From the beginning, I have to admit, this case puzzled me," I said. "Mostly because of the timing of the murder. How was it possible that nobody was nearby at the time of Mr. Lawton's death? As you all now know, I had been called in by Mrs. Lawton to see who had stolen the pearls, and, in accordance with this, I had charted the movements of everyone about the house in case someone took the opportunity to check on the pearls and reveal where they were hidden.

"According to my notes, everyone was far away from the study when we heard the scream. But how could that be possible, when surely someone had to be there, someone had to slit Mr. Lawton's throat?

"That was my first point of difficulty, and my greatest. There were two other matters, the first of which was the locked door. I did not understand that. A locked door is only useful if one is trying to establish, perhaps, a burglar coming in through a window. Yet a violent case like this made it clear to me that this could not be a common burglary—and the most valuable items that someone might have heard of and wish to steal—the pearls—had already been taken. Besides which, the windows were too small for an adult person to get into the room through that means, and I could not fathom someone reaching through the window and having Mr. Lawton draw close enough to have his throat slit, not even taking into account that Mr. Lawton was found nowhere near the window.

"The third point was the odd bit of rubber I found at the crime scene. It didn't seem to go to anything. I could not learn what it could be a part of, for it went with nothing in the room. It did not fit with any article of clothing, so it had not been torn from the murderer's outfit as they moved about the room.

"All in all, it seemed to me that the person who had stolen the pearls must be the person who had murdered Mr. Lawton. Perhaps he had found out who had taken them—and after all, he was a rather unpleasant man by all accounts. I hate to speak ill of the dead, but I confess my first couple of days here in his presence were not pleasant ones. Hatred of such a man combined with a monetary motive seemed quite sensible to me.

"But there was something that did not sit right with me, and that was how much blood there was at the scene. There was, in fact, too much blood. In my work with Mr. Holmes, he has often relayed to me the usefulness of a doctor's knowledge, and has lent me some notebooks belonging to a friend of his who is a doctor, currently off in the wars. I knew that there was too much blood in this room for one human being. It had to be there for some other reason then—but why? To make a statement, but what sort of statement?

"I recalled what I had observed when I ran to the study door, for I was the first one there. There are, as you will notice if you go out into the hall, three statues brought from Italy by the late Mr. Lawton. But when I went into the hallway to investigate that night, I observed four.

"There was only one woman that night wearing a white dress and a white shawl who might be mistaken for one of the statues if she stood very still against the wall." I looked over at Julia. "I confronted her. And she told me…"

"There was no one there!" Julia blurted out. "I went to talk to him, to speak to him—he had us under his thumb, you see, and this whole affair with the pearls was the last straw. I couldn't bear it anymore. I came to ask him, on this holy day, to let Earnest and me go live somewhere else, away from him. But when I went to the door, there was this awful sound… the scream... and then I heard footsteps and I pressed myself up against the wall..."

She took a great, heaving breath. "But you must understand, I was quite alone! Nobody came out of the room!"

"Impossible!" Peter Lawton said, jumping to his feet. "Quite impossible!"

"That is what I thought, as well," I said. "But then I remembered that the door was locked."

"What does that have to do with anything?" George Lawton demanded.

"There was no reason for the door to be locked," I explained. "Not unless the person wanted to make it look like an outside job, a burglar—or unless they needed the door locked to give them time."

"Time?" Julia repeated.

I nodded. "Yes. With the door locked, it would take us time to get into the room, time for the room to look the way that the murderer wanted it to look—and it would stop anyone from entering the room before they heard that scream."

"But why would anyone need the room locked before the murder was committed?" Louisa asked.

"Because the murder wasn't committed when we heard the scream," I said. I held up the little piece of rubber. "It was committed earlier. That was why an attempt was then made on Miss Grant's life. Her presence in the hallway—learned about by the murderer in the process of everyone being interviewed—proved that nobody had come out of the room or was in the hallway when the scream was heard. That proved that the murder had to be committed earlier in the day, about two hours earlier, in fact. The scream was merely a distraction, a ploy to fool us."

I showed them the piece of rubber. "Does this look like anything to any of you?"

Everyone shook their heads.

"It didn't look like anything to me, either," I said. "But then Mr. Holmes told me something in his letter, and I remembered what Fanny kept saying about the scream she heard—that it was inhuman, like a pig.

"I sent my sister Mary to look down in Meryton, and indeed, she found what I had thought she might."

I held up the unused pig's bladder. "This is known as a pig's bladder, or the dying pig. It's an amusing little toy, the sort of thing I would have used to give my sister Jane a fright when we were children. As the air is released, it makes this horrible wailing sound, rather like that of a dying pig."

I demonstrated, and at once the room was filled with the same awful sound we'd heard the day before. Everyone cried out, the ladies covering their ears. Even the men winced in horror.

"That awful, wicked sound!" Fanny cried out.

"But why on earth should someone set that up to be heard?" Julia wondered. "Surely it would alert everyone to the murder. Was it not in the murderer's favor that the death should go unnoticed for as long as possible?"

"Perhaps," I said, "but in this case, the murderer needed an established time of death. We were supposed to believe that this was the sound of Mr.

Lawton dying. That way we would never think he had been murdered earlier. And the locked door would prevent anyone going inside beforehand and discovering the body."

"But who did this?" Louisa asked.

"That puzzled me for a long time. Everyone, after all, had a motive. Nobody liked Mr. Lawton. The psychology—that is, the temperament of the murderer... I had to ask myself what kind of person would murder in such a bloody and brutal fashion? Charles and Earnest were both patient men, but such patience can come from suppressing anger until it builds up and builds up and finally is unleashed in a most horrible fashion. Miss Grant had often expressed her disdain for her future father-in-law and could easily have wanted him gone to free her fiancé. George and his wife were both in need of money. Peter was a man who boasted of the laws he might or might not have broken—could murder have been among his crimes?

"Even Louisa, who asked me here, might have done so in order to keep my suspicions away from her when she committed the murder to free her husband from his servitude. Anyone, in short, could have *wanted* to committed the murder. But who really *needed* to?

"And so, we come again to the blood," I said. "I found it to be quite puzzling that someone should throw extra blood everywhere. Whatever for? Was it for dramatic effect, to scare everyone? But surely that would mean some kind of warning was being given and there was no such warning. But then, Mr. Holmes reminded me of a case he worked—a case where a word was written on the wall in blood.

"The word, *rache*, was German for revenge. It was, Mr. Holmes told me, rather dramatic and one might even say foolish to write that word. However, to the killer, the message conveyed was more important than logic. Therefore, I had to ask myself, what sort of message was being conveyed with the excess of blood?

"And then I talked with Thomas Hillford—and I knew."

Mr. Hillford looked at me in surprise. "Whatever do you mean?" he asked.

"I mean, sir, that you are the illegitimate son of Mr. Lawton. Mary has sought your family out—your mother died only weeks ago. I suspect it was in a deathbed confession, was it not, that she told you of your true father and the reason for the schism between your adoptive father Mr. Hillford and his childhood best friend, Mr. Lawton?

"It was good of him to raise you as his own. I never met Mr. Hillford, of course, but I can imagine given your strength of character and his choosing to raise you, given that you only learned of your true parentage upon your mother's death, that he was a good and upright man."

"He was a good man," Mr. Hillford said passionately. "The best of men. Most men should have cast my mother aside after what happened and left her and her child to roam the streets. Not my father. He gave me his name, treated me as his own child, gave me the best education that his money could buy. I never once suspected the truth of my parentage, not until my mother confessed as she lay dying. But how ever did you find out the truth?"

"I deduced, given that your visit was mere weeks after your mother's death, that it was her death that spurred you to visit. But why, if your father was the one who knew Mr. Lawton as a child, should it be your *mother's* death that inspired you to come here?

"Then there were the little behavioral quirks that I observed. All the Lawton sons have a habit of clenching their left hand, as do you. While I had never observed you smoking, I saw the tobacco stain upon your finger and knew you are in the habit—just as the Lawton men are. The lopsided smile and the habit of covering your mouth when you laugh... your adoptive father taught you your character, Mr. Hillford, but your biological father passed down some little physical traits, ones that you did not even realize you had inherited from him."

"And so he killed Father?" Earnest asked, sounding horrified. "For revenge?"

I shook my head. "No. I did think that, perhaps, for a moment, but again, I had been recording everyone's movements about the house. If the murderer was someone who was staying in this house, then the scream was unnecessary. All the scream did was establish a time the murder could not have been committed *before*. Surely, if one was staying in the house, it would be best to keep the room locked and let the body grow cold for as long as possible, in order to confuse further the time of death, to make one wonder at what time of day this could possibly have occurred—no one had seen Mr. Lawton all day, after all, so the murder could have happened from breakfast onward.

"Unless... unless it was a person who was not staying in the house. Who had seen Mr. Lawton that day after breakfast. Someone who needed everyone to believe that Mr. Lawton was murdered at a specific time in order to give himself an alibi.

"The blood, you see, and Mr. Hillford—that was what gave me the motive. This was a crime of blood. The murderer, against reason and logic, wanted all who saw the body to know that this was a crime not just of passion, not just of hatred, but of blood. Mr. Lawton's blood. His own flesh and blood rising up against him.

"You see, Mr. Lawton already had one illegitimate son, Mr. Hillford. He slept with his best friend's fiancé. In my experience, a man who has done something such as that once will have done it before, and will do it again. A man does not simply take advantage of a lady once and then leave it at that. It is a habit.

"And so, if Mr. Lawton had one illegitimate son, was it not possible that he had more? That he had left more than one young lady to the mercy of an uncaring and unforgiving world?

"Mrs. Hillford had been fortunate, for her husband had forgiven her and stood by her, had raised her son as his own and never breathed a word about his true parentage. But there are others who are not so lucky, others who might not have had caring fiancés, or even fiancés at all. Others who might, in fact, be lower class... for if a man dares to do such a thing with a gentleman's daughter, you can be certain that he has done it with the servant girls. For if he does not care for the standing and respect of a woman of his own ranking, why should he care for the standing of a woman below him in rank? A mere servant?"

I whirled to face Lt. Crawley. "When Louisa first told me that you were here about the pearls, I took her at her word. You yourself said that Mr. Lawton had summoned an officer here for the purpose of looking into things. Yet, when I asked Louisa to go through the day again in detail, she told me that you did not tell her you were here for the pearls. You said that you were here to inquire as to a possible theft. Louisa then merely assumed, through association, that you were here about the pearls.

"But you were not, Lt. Crawley, were you? You made up a—do pardon my French—cock and bull story, about a possible theft, knowing that Mr. Lawton was a rich man and knowing that as a concerned militia man, a servant of the law and the Empire, that Mr. Lawton would let you in. There actually being a theft in the family was merely a fortunate coincidence, one you did not even learn of until you were in the room and spoke to Mr. Lawton.

"We forget, I think... all we see is the uniform. I know that is all that my younger sisters once saw: a handsome uniform. The man himself was secondary. But we learned, painfully, that on the contrary, a man in uniform is a person first, a man first and an officer second. And officers have mothers... and fathers..."

Lt. Crawley had gone quite pale. His left hand was at his side, clenched. "You have the Lawton habits, as well," I said. "The same as your half-brothers. No wonder I had such a sense of déjà vu staying in this place. I had six men about me who all laughed the same way, smiled the same way, showed their displeasure the same way. For someone trained in observation such as myself, it was giving me quite a headache and I did not even know why.

"A simple inquiry by my sister Mary with your superior officer told me the story, Lieutenant. He left your mother to suffer terribly. What he did to her was unforgivable."

"What did he do?" Louisa asked quietly.

"Mary Crawley was a parlor maid in this house when Mr. Lawton was growing up. He got her pregnant and refused to provide for her. Her pregnancy was discovered and she was put out of the house. She had to turn to walking the streets, as one might say, in order to provide for herself and her son.

"It was quite lucky for her boy, Henry, that one of her clients was able to pull some strings and get him into the militia, provide him with a recommendation. I am certain that few people knew the truth of his background—and your superior officer could only tell me that she was, well, what she was, and had got that way through the behavior of a gentleman in whose house she had been a maid.

"She must have suffered greatly. And when you learned that you were to be stationed in Meryton, you saw your chance. You had a good reputation, had been a commendable soldier. There had been a rash of petty thefts in the area recently. It would be child's play to gain access to Mr. Lawton. To slit the throat of an ailing, elderly man is nothing for a strong man such as yourself.

"But suspicion could not fall upon you, so you rigged up your little pig's bladder. I fancy you had it tied to a string that led outside the window. A pull upon the string—using one of those little knots that are designed to come undone when you pull—and the unearthly wail would alert everyone in the house to the exact time Mr. Lawton had been killed.

"Placing yourself as the investigating party, though, that was hubris. I suppose you thought that it would help you finger one of the family members as the guilty party. All of them had motive. Mr. Lawton was, after all, quite the unpleasant character. And I must admit that most criminals I have met in my time have an overestimation of their own cleverness. I have only met one who has managed to be worthy of the respect to which she afforded herself, and you are certainly not on her level."

Everyone was staring openmouthed either at myself or at Lt. Crawley.

"A military man," Fanny breathed, disbelieving.

"I must say," Peter began, then paused, then started again, "I must say, Miss Bennet, that is quite—

well, let us just say that I am most deeply mired in admiration for you."

I looked steadily at Lt. Crawley, who had been growing redder in the face this entire time. "Well, sir?" I asked.

"You damned woman!" he burst out. "You're a damnable woman, and I'm glad he's dead! You should have seen how she suffered! The way the men treated her, what it did to her body, her youth! She died sick and in the worst pain your selfish little minds can imagine, all of you brought up in wealth. Oh, yes, he was a bastard of a man, but at least he provided for you, all of you, even when you didn't deserve it and squandered his money. He gave her not a cent, used her and then left her to die a slow death. Yes, I'm quite glad he's dead, and I'm glad that I was the one who got to do it!"

Everyone was filled with astonishment at this outburst, and Lt. Crawley took advantage of it. He dashed through the door, making clearly for the back entrance.

"Mr. Darcy!" I called out, for I had planned for this. Criminals often try to run, at least in Mr. Holmes' and my experience.

There was the sound of a cry, and then a scuffle. Everyone hurried to the window to see Mr. Darcy, leading some policemen, apprehending Lt. Crawley.

"I thought it best to have my associate Mr. Darcy fetch some lawmen to have them handy. There will be an inquest, I'm afraid. I must apologize for the scandal."

"I don't suppose there shall be any way to avoid it?" George asked hopefully.

Louisa gave a very unladylike snort. "My dear George, why on earth should the man go out of his way to spare our feelings?"

"But who took the pearls, then?" Julia wondered aloud. "I thought for certain that whoever had murdered Mr. Lawton had taken them."

"That was quite a lucky chance for Lt. Crawley," I said. "To have something of great value actually stolen from the house, and to have it clearly be a member of the family—it was almost certain, therefore, at least in his mind, that one of the family must have murdered Mr. Lawton for those pearls."

"But who took them?"

Charles cleared his throat. "I did."

I turned and smiled at him. "Was it you? I thought so. Your habit of stroking the teapot on the mantelpiece as you walked by was quite telling."

"Is that where he hid them?" Earnest exclaimed.

"Yes. It was a decorative piece with a lid so no one could see inside it, and nobody would think anyone had hidden something inside it. People tend to hide things of value in a safe, or somewhere in their bedroom—Mr. Holmes has done a most interesting study of how people feel their bedrooms are their safe place and therefore hide valuables in there, particularly valuables they do not wish anyone to know about." I looked again at Charles. "That was clever of you to put it there, I doubt if it had not been for the habit of stroking it I should have guessed."

"I didn't wish to do anything with them," Charles said. "I only wished to keep them safe. Father so easily gave into Peter, and I knew George was in dire financial straits. I feared he would give one or both of them the pearls—and they were to be used to maintain this property. I couldn't bear to let the grounds fall into disrepair because Father threw good money after bad."

Peter laughed. "Can't hold that against you, brother. I'll be the first to admit that I'm not the kind of man you can depend on, at least in the past. I do hope you'll give me the chance to prove to you that I'm here to stay and turn myself around. I've got into a fair amount of trouble overseas and I feel as though I've had quite enough excitement for a lifetime."

"Throwing good money after bad," George grumbled, obviously quite put out. "As if…"

I did not bother to listen to the rest of what he said. "If there is nothing else… I'm afraid that I must get back to my family. I am certain that I shall see you all at the inquest." I turned to Louisa. "I am sorry to have spent such time with you with a cloud hanging over us. I do hope I shall visit you again soon under more joyful circumstances."

"You must be invited to the wedding!" Julia exclaimed. "You've been so awfully good to us, Miss Bennet, you must attend."

"I feel rather as if a shadow's been lifted," Earnest said, and indeed, he looked healthier almost, standing up straighter. I felt confident that now that his father was no longer constantly berating him, Earnest would be able to come into his own and be the man that, ironically, his father had always wanted him to be.

"It would give me great happiness to be able to attend your wedding," I told them, feeling much lighter myself now that the case had been solved.

And—although I did hate to brag to others, I could at least admit it to myself—I had done it all with only the slightest of assistance from Mr. Holmes, and of course Mary's helpful errand running.

It seemed I truly had the makings of a detective after all.

Chapter Eight:
First Class

It was only proper that I should thank Mr. Darcy for his help.

"You rather put yourself out there on my behalf," I told him, "and I appreciate your assistance. I could not possibly have gotten the police to listen to me on my own." While I liked to think that I was forceful enough to persuade many people, I doubted the police would have followed me had I been the one to request their presence in catching a murderer.

"Certainly." Mr. Darcy paused. "I'm not averse to helping you out in such a fashion again, should the need arise. I must admit that when I first met you, I was unsure as to your character. You seemed... quite assured in your immediate judgment of others. Yet now I find you to possess great patience and discernment."

"I'm not certain that I'm worthy of such praise," I told him. "I am certain that I still have much to learn."

"This was a case, from what you have told me of it, that required a bit of psychological deduction as well as deduction of the facts," Mr. Darcy replied. "Every single person in that house had a motive for killing Mr. Lawton and yet you did not jump to conclusions about any of them. You reviewed the facts and allowed that to supply your theory and you did not make an assumption about anyone's character—otherwise you might have assumed, as did all the others, that a military man is above question."

"Mr. Wickham taught me that military men are men first," I said quietly. "But I thank you. I have often allowed myself to fall into an erroneous opinion of someone based upon a poor first impression and my own hasty conclusions. I am glad to hear that you think I am improving." I smiled, then, unable to resist teasing him a bit. "You've gotten rather more tolerable yourself."

Mr. Darcy chuckled. "Yes, well, I was rather rude to you upon our first meeting. Perhaps we both have our own little prejudices."

I bade him good day and upon my return home to Longbourn. I found Father much recovered from his illness and Mother still in rather a tizzy both over this and over the news of the murder. I was obliged to stay on for a few extra days in order to get both of my parents settled to everyone's satisfaction.

On one of the days, I received a letter from Mr. Holmes. I had written to tell him all of the facts and how the murderer had been apprehended. His letter was short, and as follows:

Miss Bennet,
I am pleased to hear that you were able to solve the case. I did not doubt your ability, only your faith in yourself. Well done. You're turning into a first-class detective.

I hope I shall see you darken my door again soon. Progress is being made here.

~ H

It gave me a thrill to have such a compliment, and in writing, from Mr. Holmes. Indeed, this entire case had given me a strong dose of confidence that I hadn't even known that I needed. I had depended upon Mr. Holmes ever since I had started my detective work, and now I had proven to both him and myself that I could handle cases standing on my own two feet. It gave me quite a rush.

On our last day at Longbourn before we returned to London, I was presenting Mary with the facts of the case to see if she might be able to solve it. She was already acquainted with some of the facts, having fetched information for me while I was stuck at the Lawton house, but the identity of the murderer had yet to become common knowledge—just that a murder had been committed. I had little doubt that all the facts would be splashed across the papers soon. It was a pity, but hopefully it was the beginning of the end of the misery the Lawton children had been subjected to.

Mary and I were discussing things when a maid entered. "If you'll pardon me, Miss Bennet, there's a gentleman here to see you. Two of them, actually. A Mr. Lawton and a Mr. Hillford."

Mary and I both stood as the gentlemen entered. "Good day, sirs," I said. "How can I be of assistance?"

"I was hoping that I might have the pleasure of speaking to you alone?" Peter Lawton said.

Well, he was bold, so at least he had that in his favor. I sighed inwardly and indicated for Mary to leave the room. She did so, asking Mr. Hillford of his profession and suggesting a turn about the gardens.

There was no use in prolonging the inevitable. When a man gets it into his head that he is going to propose, I thought, it is best that one allow him to get on with it.

"Miss Bennet," Peter Lawton said, "it has struck me that throughout this awful matter with my family, you have behaved in a most admirable manner. I am not the kind of man who wishes for a conventional wife, one who simpers and giggles and thinks only of children and needlework. I would like a wife of strong character, of unusual and daring character—a woman who is, one might say, possessed of a steel backbone.

"I had thought I should look for a wife when I am more settled back here in England, but when a woman such as yourself comes into a man's life, a man must take advantage while he can. I know that we have not yet seen much of one another, but I have been impressed enough by what I have seen. It would honor me greatly if you would take my hand in marriage."

"Mr. Lawton," I said, "I am flattered by your proposal—and that it was my help in this case that caused you to think so highly of me. However, I must admit that nothing short of the deepest affection could compel me to accept an offer of marriage. I am in no need of a husband. My work is my passion, and I'm afraid I cannot possibly give it up for any person.

"Besides, Mr. Lawton, while you are currently impressed with me... I think that we would be ill-suited for one another." Not to mention, I could never marry a man as ne'er-do-well as Peter Lawton. But there was no need for me to be rude.

Peter Lawton bowed. "As you say, Miss Bennet. It is your choice."

Thank goodness there were no hysterics.

When I opened the door, I was little surprised to see Mother standing there. She—and the rest of my family, I admit—had an awful habit of listening at doors. "Oh! Lizzy, I heard there was a young man asking for you."

"Mother, this is Mr. Peter Lawton. Sir, my mother, Mrs. Bennet."

"How do you do." Peter Lawton bowed to her. "I was just on my way out."

I came to stand by Mother as Peter exited. "Well," she said. "I must say he handled the rejection well. Good work on your part, my dear."

I frowned. "You are not upset that I refused him?" I would have thought that my mother would jump at the chance to see me married. Once I had thought it was because she wanted to get rid of me, but I now understood that it was because she was scared for me and wanted me to have security and be taken care of.

Mother snorted. "Dear Lizzy, you can do so much better than that. He is not nearly good enough for you."

I have to admit that I was outright gaping at her. "Not... good enough for me?"

Mother turned and looked at me, and for the first time in my life, I could see pride in her eyes as she looked upon me. Mother had never been proud of me before. "You just helped out a family and probably saved one of them from an unfair hanging and brought a most gruesome murderer to justice. I should think you'd deserve a man who possessed just as much mettle as you."

I could not help myself. I hugged my mother tightly. She might not fully approve of my detective work, but to know that at least once, I had made her proud, and that she thought I deserved only the best of men—it made me feel like I was truly her daughter.

As I pulled back, Mother added, "I did see Mary discussing law with another young man. Did he accompany Mr. Lawton?"

"Yes, that is Mr. Hillford. He's studying to be a lawyer."

"They did seem to be getting on rather well. I overheard him offer to lend Mary some of his law books."

I knew that gleam in Mother's eyes. "Honestly, Mother, they've only just met. I wouldn't be so eager to marry her off."

"It's Mary, my dear, you know that out of all of you, she'll have the hardest time of it. Always disappearing into her books."

I shook my head ruefully. Already we were anticipating proposals for Kitty and Lydia. It would be nice to keep at least one of my sisters around for a bit longer, especially the one who was turning into quite the apprentice for me.

On our journey back to London, I inquired about Mr. Hillford to Mary.

"He has asked if he might call upon us in London," Mary said. "He is studying to be a lawyer there, you know."

"And what do you think of him?" I asked.

"I think that I enjoy conversing with him." Mary shrugged. "Perhaps I shall think more of him in time. But tell me, what are the other facts of the case?"

I smiled. At least for now, Mary was more interested in solving cases than in potential suitors.

I did not expect much when I got home to London. Kitty and Lydia had much to say, of course, about the balls I had missed out on and the theatre shows I must see. They were also full of praise for various men, which was not unexpected.

"And how are they truly?" I asked Jane after hugging her. I had missed my dearest and favorite sister so. Little Tom, my nephew, was quite happy to see me, as well, and I held him for a bit before we had to put him down for a nap.

"Quite well, but I find myself almost hoping that someone will propose. I much preferred a quieter house," Jane admitted. "But there is a letter for you, from Mr. Holmes. He wishes for you to visit him at Baker Street at your earliest convenience."

"I'll go at once."

My trip to Baker Street was late, but I did not mind. Many people were still out and about. When I entered the flat, I found it to be in complete disarray. "Mr. Holmes?"

"Oh, good, you're here," he said, in a tone that suggested I was late to some meeting or other. "I've got it!"

"Got what?" I asked. This flat was really a complete mess, it was going to take me forever to straighten everything up.

"Moriarty," Mr. Holmes said. He smiled at me, triumph gleaming in his eyes. "I've got him."

"How? Has he been apprehended?"

Mr. Holmes shook his head. "No, Miss Bennet." Then he said, as if that explained everything—and perhaps, to him, it did, "Mathematics."

THE END

About the Author

Amelia works as a librarian and lives in an idyllic Cotswold village in England with Darcy, her Persian cat. She has been a Jane Austen fan since childhood but only in later life did she discover the glory and gory of a cozy mystery book. She has drafted many different cases for Holmes and Bennet to solve together.

Visit www.amelialittlewood.com for more details.

Made in United States
Orlando, FL
13 February 2025